My Home, My Family, My Country:

A Story of Triumph

S. Lee Cupit

PublishAmerica
Baltimore

First printing

Hardcover 978-1-4560-6933-9
Softcover 978-1-4560-6932-2
PUBLISHED BY PUBLISHAMERICA, LLLP
www.publishamerica.com
Baltimore

Printed in the United States of America

Dedication

I dedicate this book to my mother Doris Lester Betner, my three daughters, Sharlyn, Lori and Kelly, son-in-law Leander, my grandchildren SaVonne, Edward, Christopher, Marc, Joy, Joshua and Janae, and my siblings, Lois, Mary, Cleora, Doris, Bruce and James and family all who have inspired and encouraged me.

Table of Contents

Introduction

This story of Freedom was born out of a desire to share in our yearly black history program at Delaware Valley Baptist Church, James L. Betner, pastor. I wanted to participate in the (Share a thon). This program was open to all and it could be poetry, drama, song or reading, published or an original work. It could be past or present day history.

When the announcement was made at church, I prayed because I wanted to be a part of it. I thought of a poem I had written when in undergrad school, but did not remember where it was. That evening after church I prayed and asked God for wisdom on writing a new poem or a short story. As I sat before my laptop the words just began to flow. An anointing to write from my heart about our history flowed through me.

The story is fiction but it touches on the many lives of a people made into slaves by greed and unrighteousness.

The story grew and grew so much that I only read a brief excerpt for the event. One of the many things that really showed me that it was the anointing of God on me to write this was Mama Sara's song. As I was writing it just flowed with the melody and all. I found myself singing it as I wrote.

The story lets us know that in all the darkness we might face in our lives, God loves us in the midst of it. As we move on in forgiveness we can say, "yet in all these things we are more than conquerors through Him who loved us."

**Romans 8:37*

Chapter 1
Innocence Stolen

Sara ran happily down the path following a red ribbon.
"What is this?" She said as she followed it.

Suddenly she was scooped up by a rough looking white man. He put his hand over her mouth and carried her to a waiting boat. There were many people in the boat from her village and other villages.

"Where were they taking them?"

She cried but couldn't scream for her father. They were all gagged and their feet and hands were shackled. They finally reached the ship and were forced aboard and put in the hole.

There were so many people! It was so crowded, what was she to do?

The journey on the ship was horrible. Many jumped overboard in despair of not seeing home and family again. Most were whipped and abused. All were shackled together and made to lie in their own waste in the bottom of the ship.

The days seemed to pass very slowly, and Sara lost track of

time. She hardly ever came up on deck except when someone was being whipped or punished as an example to the rest of them.

What was Sara to do? What could she do?

She endured; she survived the journey, through high winds, scorching heat and rough seas. Sara survived through the crying and dying of so many. She had to survive so that she could one day possibly see her family again.

"Get up!" The slave makers shouted as they threw water on them and laughed.

They all got soaked, and Sara blinked and wiped the water from her face. She looked wide eyed and blinked again as they were brought up on deck again. It was a bright day and the change from being in the hole made her eyes hurt.

They came into port and were off loaded.

"Where is this place? Where is my home?" She wondered, as she looked behind her and saw no familiar land-mark.

Fear gripped her heart!

"Where is my mama?" She sobbed.

Unlike some of the people who were kidnapped to be sold as slaves, Sara had heard of white men before. There had been some missionaries who had come to her village before she was born. Her parents told her that they had named her for the wife of the missionary. She didn't understand these men though. They were rough, and uncivilized. She understood some of the things they said. They kept calling them savages.

"They were the ones acting like savages!" She thought.

Sara was stripped and made to parade naked on the auction block. She was sold like a sack of potatoes to Massa Charles Bolene. She worked in his cotton fields all of her sojourn as a slave.

She married or jumped the broom as it was sometimes called, Henry Botian, a man who had been a free black man. He could read and write. He had worked on ships in the far north.

Henry worked along-side another free black man named Joshua.

Joshua told Henry, "The cold is too much for me, I'm going west to California where I can build ships and feel the warmth of the sun."

He sent word to Henry that it was like home. Henry decided to follow him there. On his way he was taken and sold as a slave to Massa Bolene.

Henry and Sara had eight children, three boys and five girls; all of whom were sold and taken away. Her heart broke with each child who was taken and sold. She prayed night and day for them. She never saw them again!

Sara and Henry were old when freedom came. Old by the standards of workers in cotton fields, she was thirty and he was forty. They looked much older from the beatings, hard work, little food and shelter.

But they had come to know the Lord and were able to endure and have hope.

And they were thankful that they were allowed to stay together on the same plantation. Many whole families were sold off one by one.

The year of freedom Sara and Henry had a son. This one was for them! They were sure that the Lord had given him to them to make up for the pain of losing all the other children to slavery. They named him Freedom. They told him all about their home across the large water; and hoped that one day he would go and find his people there.

Freedom was very smart. He learned Mama Sara's language and the language of the new country, as his parents called America. Poppa Henry taught him his numbers.

Henry's job had been keeping track of all the cotton sacks making sure that they were counted properly so Massa wasn't shortchanged. If anything went wrong the slaves were whipped.

There was Miss Annie Bolene, another former slave who worked in the house and could read and write. Mistress Bolene took a liking to Annie and taught her. She was able to help Mistress Bolene with the house and reading to the children.

Miss Annie later became a teacher for everyone who wanted to learn. The one thing they all did was help each other. They understood the importance of freedom and being able to read and write and build a life for themselves and their families.

Everyone knew about some former slaves who were so dependent on the Massa that they became servants for life with nothing changing for them. They had no hope of anything ever being better.

Henry and Sara were determined to have a better life for themselves and Freedom. There were many freed slaves who felt the same way. They knew that it wouldn't be easy, but they remembered the whippings, hunger and separation from their families and were convinced that God would keep them.

Some stayed on the outskirts of the same town; others on former slave owners land doing sharecropping. It wasn't an easy living and some said it was just as bad as slavery. But many knew there was a difference. They could come and go as they pleased. They were working for their own families.

It was unfortunate that many landowners were cruel and greedy.

But as Poppa Henry said one Sunday at church, "The Lord has given us strength to endure all that has come upon us, and he will not leave us now that he turned our captivity around."

Over their remaining years, Henry and Sara taught Freedom

what his name meant and told him how he should depend on God for everything. Mama Sara wanted him to know her history and his. She told him that she was free born and in her own country and village with her own parents when she was lured by the red ribbon and kidnapped. Mama Sara wanted him to understand that they were people with lives, hopes and dreams just like the white folks.

"Never hang your head and be ashamed of who you are," she always told him. "You have a country, home and family who love you and hope to see you one day."

Freedom grew strong and confident in knowing that God had a plan and purpose for his life. He was determined that he would make his parents proud of him and would one day find their home and go there.

His parents were sharecroppers. They had a small little air-lighted house. You could see through the wall boards and roof. Freedom worked hard in the cotton field along- side them, and in the little potato patch. It seemed like there was no time to rest. They barely made enough to feed themselves.

Freedoms' parents were gentle hearted people, and always encouraged him saying, "It's not gonna always be like it is now."

Henry, Sara and Freedom all attended a small wooden house church, along with most of the neighboring sharecroppers. They carried their own stools to and from service. Their pastor Rev. William Jones was a circuit rider and was with them only one Sunday a month. They had services without him the rest of the month. There was only one nearly complete Bible. Most people had a few pages of a book. But they cherished it and faithfully read what they could.

Freedom was the best reader, so he would read the scripture and the deacon would line the song that they sang. They all had the opportunity to give their testimony of God's goodness to them from their forced journey over the big water and through the end of slavery. He loved going to church. Freedom loved reading the Bible and praying. He was told by everyone he would be a preacher one day. Freedom wasn't sure that was what he wanted to do. But he didn't want to disappoint his parents.

Mama Sara got up one morning fixed breakfast of biscuits and gravy and coffee; sat down and died. It didn't make any sense; and Freedom and his father were left in shock, disbelief and shaken. Poppa Henry began to withdraw. He no longer worked the field with Freedom, nor did he talk much anymore.

One day Freedom came in from the field and found his father dead.

Mama Sissy, the midwife and only doctor they had said, "It was a broken heart!"

"How is that possible?" asked Freedom.

After the death and burial of his father, Freedom decided to leave and find his own way. Although the church members, who were like family to him were sad; they understood his need to get away from the place that held such painful memories. All the mamas gave him advice about safety and the men warned him about being fool hearty, and forgetting that men had evil hearts all over the country.

Chapter 2
Searching For A Place to Belong

There was a freight train over in the next town, that Massa Bolene used to ship his cotton on. Freedom determined in his heart to catch it the next night and head on up north. After putting what little he had in an old quilt his mama had made he tied it with a rope and slung it over his back. He took the few cans of beans and a few hard biscuits and started on his journey. He had an old jacket mama Sara had made and lined with some of her quilt material to keep him warm.

There was an old song that his mama loved to sing as she was working in the house or field and he loved to hear her sing it.

"You cover me with your love. You lift me up when I am down. You are my God, my fathers' God. I love you Lord, You are my God. "

Freedom's face was wet as he hummed the song walking to the neighboring town to hop the freight.

As he was nearing the town he saw a group of white men in front of the station. He remembered his father's warnings to him about being out alone and what to do if he saw a group of white men. He knew from experience about the men who had gone missing and later found lynched or beaten to death. He took a detour around where they were. He quietly went down the alley around the back and started down the tracks. He would jump on the freight train when it stopped for water. He wondered how long it would be before things changed like mama Sara said they would.

He saw an open door and was about to run up to jump on when he saw two white men in the car. They were hard looking. He let that car pass and jumped on the next one. There was a man asleep in the corner. He got in the opposite corner and watched and prayed. Finally Freedom couldn't keep his eyes open and fell asleep. He was startled awake by the sound of men arguing. He opened his eyes and sure enough there were three men with their backs to him on the other side of the car arguing.

They had been playing cards and someone said, "You cheated me for the last time!"

Freedom didn't know what to do. He didn't want to get involved, for fear of being lynched. The train was pulling slowly into the yard. He didn't know where, but he decided to jump off and maybe get in another car or walk awhile and jump the next train. Freedom eased himself as quietly as possible to the door and lowered himself out. He was about to call it a day when he saw a car with straw on the floor.

He peeked in and saw animals. He thought, "Now this should be safe! They won't attack me in my sleep or feel that I am not good enough to ride with them."

He hopped on and got in the far corner making kind of a barrier between him and the animals.

The train came to a halt and he could hear the yard detective hitting the side of the cars warning anyone in them to get off or be arrested. Someone peered into the car but mumbled something about animals and closed the door back and left. He also heard the men yelling who were in the other car.

"Thank you Jesus," he breathed.

The train started up again and he rode all the way to the next town. He got off and avoiding as many white men as possible, he walked looking for a place to stay the night. He saw a rooming house and there was a black woman hanging clothes on the line.

Mary Steward was her name, and she was kind enough to give him breakfast for chopping wood. Mary owned the rooming house. She had worked for years doing laundry and cleaning house and had saved enough to buy the little house. It was very small, but it had three small rooms. She had partitioned part of the sitting room into two small bedrooms.

She made a modest living. Freedom had never met anyone like her before. She was tall compared to Mama Sara. She was fair-skinned and had black hair with a hint of brown. Her eyes were brown like his mama's. She was a full woman, but not fat. She had full lips and hips. He smiled to himself when he thought of that.

He stayed a few days helping with chores, but was determined to go on up north and learn the ship building trade like his poppa.

"One day I would like to go to California," Freedom said.

"California?" Mary asked, "That's the other end of the world!"

Freedom laughed.

"My Poppa told me that he had known a man when he was a freeman, who went to California. He got word back to him that it was near as he could remember of home. Poppa always wanted to go there and see for himself. And since he never had the chance, I'll go for him."

Mary looked and listened. She thought to herself, that she had never met a man like Freedom in her life. Freedom was about 6'2, like his father and his people. He was slender and yet muscular. He had a high forehead with gentle dark brown eyes. Freedom had a beautiful dark brown complexion, with a nice broad nose, and thin lips. He had a beautiful smile and white near perfect teeth. He carried himself well. Freedom was a hard worker, even tempered and a gentle man. He talked reverently and lovingly of the Lord's goodness.

Mary didn't try to interfere with his plan. She fixed him some food and wrapped it in one of her large cloth napkins for his journey.

Mary did ask Freedom, "When you reach the shipyards, will you remember me and write?"

Freedom smiled and said, "Yes Ma'am, I will!"

"Be careful! Mary said. There are many men who used to be slave catchers; who are catching people and selling them as servants to former slave owners."

"I will. God bless you Miss Mary!" Freedom answered.

They said their goodbyes and he took a back road to the railroad tracks that Mary had told him about.

He hopped the freight and got settled in a far corner where no one could see him, but he would see anyone getting on. He thought about Mary and smiled. He had told her that he would write to her. She had put a tablet and pencil in with the food. Now he would write to her for sure.

Freedom rode for many days, jumping off and on as the need arose. Finally, the freight was coming close to New York and he knew that he must jump off before they arrived at the yard.

Freedom waited until the train slowed a little more and stood so that he could see where he would land. He made sure no one was around and eased down to a squatting position and jumped and rolled into some brush. He lay there for a moment and heard voices of men jumping off the train down from him.

Since Freedom didn't want any trouble in this new place he waited patiently until their voices died down as they continued on their way. Finally, Freedom slowly stood up and made his way further down the slope to a dirt road. He followed it looking for any place he could spend the night.

He came upon a campfire and the smell of coffee. He walked up and saw several rail-riding men around the fire drinking coffee and one was cooking what looked and smelled like ham and eggs. They looked up at him and nodded. They were all former slaves and had been on the rails for a long time. They offered him coffee if he had his own cup. He did and said thanks. They had each brought something to contribute to the meal.

They talked most of the night about their lives since slavery ended and about family left behind while they were looking for a better life for them. One man named Junior; short compared to Freedom, and with a slight limp; was low in his spirit. He told of how he had left home three years ago and that he had only been able to send a little money back home in all of those years.

"I reckon I should have stayed home with them but now I fear it's too late to go back with nothing. My children are big and don't hardly know me. They see their momma struggling every day, and I am gone so they can have a better life!"

"With so little work there's hardly any money to send home to them. How's it better with me here jumping from train to train in little towns hardly getting enough for me to eat?" Junior asked.

They all had stories of lost hope, hard life and missing family most of all.

Freedom said, "I don't have no family, at least none that I know. My momma and poppa died but they did have children during slavery that was sold out from under them. I don't reckon I'll ever meet them or hope to know them. I'm going to the ship yards to learn how to build ships like my poppa did and one day go on to California."

"I hope to marry one day a fine lady named Miss Mary. But now learning ship building is first."

They continued to talk into the wee hours. Finally they drifted off as the fire embers glowed and started to die.

Freedom roused himself and went on his way. He knew it was better to be on his own than in a group. He got a little job chopping wood and cleaning a stable on a farm in New York. He stayed for over a month saving what little he got.

Freedom was known as an honest hard working colored man. He kept to himself on the farm, did his work and didn't complain. He made friends with the surrounding farms' colored workers. Some had come like him looking for a better life for themselves and their families. Others had always been in them parts. And to Freedom's surprise he learned there were slaves up north too.

Chapter 3
Poppa Henry's Home

One morning he knew that he needed to leave. He had overheard Mr. Langdon and a visiting friend talking about how much money could be made by selling former slaves to land owners in the south.

"They have no papers and all you have to do is say that they are a threat to decent folk," Mr. Langdon told his friend.

They planned to get him the next evening. Freedom got up before daylight and eased away taking all of his things, including the little money he had sewed into the lining of his jacket Mama Sara made for him. Freedom was off. He had talked to other hands in the neighboring farms and learned the best way to go to the far north. They also told him that it was very cold and if he didn't have decent clothes or shoes he would freeze to death.

Freedom had paid John Tulane's wife from the nearby farm to make him a pair of heavy pants using quilt material and another jacket big enough to cover the one his mama made.

Mrs. Langdon had given him a pair of her husband's old boots; warning him, "Don't let him find out about it."

Freedom had gone to the smithy and he put some leather on the bottom of the boots and gave him some for inside the boots. He had old socks and one pair of good gloves that the ma'am gave him for the outside work he did. Freedom knew that he would need food because he couldn't stop at every farm along the way. They would want to know where he worked before and he was a feared Mr. Langdon would come after him.

Freedom was on his way he carried his quilt over his shoulder with all of his possessions. He hitched a ride on a wagon with his friend Fred who worked a small farm near him. Fred was a freeman and married with three daughters.

He told Freedom, "If my daughters were older I would let you marry one of them."

Freedom said, "Thank you, but I got a promise waiting for me."

Fred said, "It's hard living in between larger farms. They are always trying to force you out so that they could have your land."

Fred had been there bouts for over ten years and his father's family before him since before the independence.

He said, "I helped build this country and we're not leaving."

That was what Freedom wanted, his own home, family all the things his momma and poppa slaved for and lost children for. He was willing to work hard to get it.

Freedom and Fred rode silently for a long way over the rough back road.

Finally they came to a fork and Fred said, "Go on yonder for about a couple days and you'll see some water, follow the river till you get to the mill. I got a friend named Johnny that works there last I heard. Tell him I sent you and he will help you find work and a place to stay."

The two men shook hands and Freedom eased himself off the wagon.

"Tell your missus and gals farewell for me."

"God bless you all for helping me."

Fred said, "God speed you on your journey safely." And he rode on.

Freedom started on his journey to the shipyards. It was just like Fred said, and he found Johnny. He was a tall lanky colored man built kind of like Freedom even the shape of his head. Freedom looked at him a long time before approaching him.

"Scuse me sir, but is your name Johnny?" Freedom asked.

"Why yes suh, and who is it asking?" answered Johnny.

"My name is Freedom. Fred down yonder said that I was to look you up for some work and a place to stay while I'm on my way to the ship yards."

"Well, how's ole Fred and his family doin?" Asked Johnny.

"Theys fine and send their hellos." Freedom answered.

"You can come home with me, it's nigh unto suppa time." Johnny said.

Freedom followed Johnny thinking to himself how he reminded him of his poppa. They arrived at his house. It wasn't much more than the old house Freedom lived in with his momma and poppa. He wondered how Johnny managed in the cold weather with so many wide planks on the walls and ceiling. He could see the places he had patched the walls by putting paper or cloth between the planks trying to keep the cold out.

There was a small wooden table and two chairs. There was also a cot against one wall and a small wood burning stove over near the middle of the room. He had a shelf on the wall with a few things and a wooden box on the floor with his stores in.

Johnny said, "Make yourself to home while I fix us some food."

He added some wood chips from his box and paper scraps to the stove and the fire kindled. He went out back and came in with a pot.

"Sista James, from the church made me a pot of her beans." Johnny said.

He put it on the stove to warm. Johnny showed Freedom out back where he had dug a deep ditch to keep his food. He had an outhouse and a pump out there also.

"The owner of the mill lets me live here. You can stay for a while until you find your own place."

They sat down to eat the beans. They used metal plates like Momma Sara had but rougher and big spoons. Since Freedom had his own cup he used that one to drink from.

"Fine looking cup," Johnny said.

"My momma bought it with her hard earned money when I was a boy." Freedom said.

"You have a fine momma." Johnny replied.

The men gave thanks for their food, ate and shared memories of their journey in the new land.

Turns out that Johnny was from the same people as Poppa Henry, he remembered some of the same things that his poppa had told him about his home. The two men looked at each other in astonishment. They grieved silently for the great loss of family and home to this land.

Finally, Johnny asked Freedom, "What shipyards are you looking for?"

"What do you mean?" asked Freedom. "My Poppa worked in shipyards building ships up north, he said. I am trying to find them so I can learn how to build ships too."

"What I mean Freedom is there are ship yards on the other side of the river and further up north."

Freedom stared. He didn't know where the place was or if it mattered as long as he learned how to build ships. He told Johnny what he was thinking and the men decided that the next day Freedom would cross the river on the raft and look for work. Johnny told Freedom what to expect and how to act when he crossed over the river.

"The men that work there although they are freemen must treat the white men like they are better than them. They don't look them in the eye. Always say yes suh and never complain whatever the job is."

Freedom said, "Just like down home. I'll be alright."

"Cross back over the river before dark. Many people have drowned trying to cross in the dark. If they say you must work until dark leave. There are other shipyards." Johnny said.

Chapter 4
A Mans Gotta Work

Freedom crossed over on the raft. He didn't have to pay if he got the job cause the owners paid for the rafts men to bring workers cross the river. Freedom walked and watched the men working. It was a good sight to him seeing men working hard and not begging. He walked up to a colored man getting a ladle of water and asked him where he could go to get work. The man's name was Aaron.

He told Freedom, "Go over yonder to that house with the shelf at the window and ask for Mr. Burn."

Freedom walked over to the small house, which was the office and approached the open window.

"Scuse me suh," said Freedom.

"What do you want, why ain't you working?" Asked Mr. Burn.

"I'm looking for Mr. Burn to get some work," said Freedom.

"Turn around walk back some, now turn. Well you look strong. This is hard work boy and we don't want anyone who is afraid of work," said Mr. Burn.

"I ain't afraid of hard work." Freedom replied.

"Okay, go see Jiles over there with the black suspenders, he will get you started. You got to be here every morning at five o'clock and work until five in the evening everyday but Sunday. Is that clear? If you miss a day you'll be fired." said Mr. Burn.

"Yes suh, Mr. Burn," said Freedom.

He ran over to where Jiles was talking to another worker. Now Jiles was a fair skinned colored man. At first Freedom thought that he was a white man until he got closer.

Freedom said, "Scuse me, Jiles, Mr. Burn told me to come see you about work and that I was to come in every morning at five and leave at five except Sunday I'm off."

Jiles whirled around to see who had the nerve to call him Jiles and not Mr. Jiles and to say when he was working and when he was off.

"Boy who do you think you're calling Jiles? You address me as Mr. Jiles and I tell you if you got a job and when you work and don't is that clear?"

"I beg your pardon, Mr. Jiles, but Mr. Burns told me to see Jiles not Mr. Jiles. He also told me the days I would work and be off. Now if you want me to go back over to him and tell him that you changed them I will be pleased to."

"Oh, said, Jiles, a smart boy are you huh?"

"No suh! I ain't no boy!

My father was a freeman shipbuilder till he was captured and sold. "He could read and write and taught me. My momma told me I am as good as any man."

Jiles was so taken aback at the gall of this poor looking colored man talking back to him sounding like an educated man that he sputtered. He grabbed Freedom by the arm and walked him away from the other workers, lest they forget who they were.

"What do you mean your father was free and worked the shipyards? All my family worked the shipyards since the country began. What was your father's name?" asked Jiles.

"Botian, Henry Botian."

Jiles just stared at him, his mouth hanging open.

He took Freedom further away from the men and said, "We will talk after work at six tonight."

"I can't stay after dark to cross over the river. I heard men have died trying to cross after dark. I' m only gonna work til five," said Freedom.

"Where are you staying across the river?" Jiles asked.

"With a man named Johnny who runs the mill." Freedom said.

"I know of him, Jiles replied. I'll come to see you tonight."

"Now come on and I'll show you where to start."

Jiles walked Freedom over to an open building like a high covered bridge. There was a lot of lumber in there being sorted, carted out and skinned. Freedom was given to Peterson the overseer who put him to work immediately learning how to sort what was needed for the day's work.

It was a lunch whistle that startled Freedom. He was busy working. He followed the men outside and there was some hot soup with fish and a piece of cornbread. It was warming and filling. Freedom went back and worked until five o'clock, then started to leave.

Peterson asked him, "Where do you think you are going?"

Freedom repeated in a slow deliberate way what Mr. Burn had told him.

Peterson said, "Go on," reluctantly.

He and the other workers wondered why Mr. Burn told him that, but no one would ever question the boss.

Freedom waited for the raft and sure enough there was the rafts man.

"Got the job?" He asked.

"Yes Suh," Freedom replied.

"Why are you leaving so early then?" Collins asked.

"Mr. Burn said for me to." Answered Freedom.

Collins stared at him suspiciously, but he didn't see anyone chasing him so he took him on across the river.

"What time you crossing in the morning?" Asked Collins.

"I have to be to work at five o'clock. Freedom answered.

"See you bright and early tomorrow," Collins said.

"Yes suh," Freedom answered.

Freedom made his way to Johnny's house. He was home warming some more of them beans. Freedom smiled.

"Smells mighty good," he said.

"Yes suh, it still does. Come on in Freedom and tell me what happened at the yards. I guess you got a job seeing you didn't come back."

"Yes suh, Johnny I got a job. Thanks to the Lord. He must of heard you say don't cross in the dark, cause Mr. Burn the boss told me to come in at five and leave at five even before I could ask to leave before dark.

Many of the workers including Jiles and Peterson were unbelieving that I got to leave early. They all got to stay until six or even seven. Well I believe the Lord heard our prayer. Let's pray and eat."

Johnny had made a hoecake and they had it with their beans.

"They were some good eatins." Freedom said with satisfaction.

"Yes suh, Johnny replied. "We got to thank Sis James on Sunday. We surely do."

"By the way Johnny, said Freedom, Jiles is coming over the river to see me this evening."

"Why?" Johnny asked.

"I don't know, he wanted me to stay until six to talk but I said that Mr. Burn told me to leave at five." Freedom answered.

"Did you get in trouble with him? Johnny asked. I heard that he is harder on the coloreds than any white man."

"I know he got mad at me when I called him Jiles. He will be here soon. I'll go out and wait for him after I help you clean up." Freedom said.

"No, Johnny said, it will be getting dark soon and you have to leave early light. Get your things ready by the door for tomorrow then wait outside."

Johnny left early also so he finished tidying up the room and got ready to lie down. It wasn't that he was inhospitable to Jiles, it had been a long hard day and he needed to sleep. He knew that Freedom was tired also. He felt bad that he had to sleep on the floor but he only had one cot. Freedom didn't seem to mind though.

Freedom sat on the door ledge waiting for Jiles. Then he heard voices coming from the river area. They were getting louder and Freedom was feeling uneasy. Then there was Jiles with two other workers. It sounded as if they had been drinking.

"There's that boy who thinks he can come to my job and tell me what his hours are going to be and disrespect me in front of the workers calling me Jiles. I want you men to teach him a lesson." Jiles said.

They started to approach the house and Freedom. Suddenly the door opened and there was Johnny with a shotgun in his hand.

"You men git right now! I will report you to the mill owner and he will let Mr. Burn know that you tried to cause trouble here. Now git!" Johnny said.

They stood still and looked from Jiles to Johnny.

Finally they said, "We need our job, we have families to take care of. You handle your own business, Mr. Jiles."

They turned and left.

"If I were you Mr. Jiles, I would go home and sleep it off and hope that the men don't report you to Mr. Burn." Johnny said.

Jiles was angry and stormed off mumbling something about it wasn't finished. Freedom looked at his retreating back and then at Johnny.

"I don't know what to say. I never expected this. Thank you for helping me. I am sorry I brought this to your home." Freedom said.

Johnny said, "Come on in and get some sleep."

Freedom looked around and then went inside and unrolled his blanket, prayed and lay down to sleep.

It seemed like he had just lain down and it was time to get up. Freedom was remembering the events of last evening. He couldn't understand Jiles' attitude towards him. He got up dressed went out back and washed his face and headed to the river. There was the raft. He greeted Collins and got on along with several others.

Collins motioned for him to come closer.

"I heard about what happened last night. I ain't going to let them men cross with me again.

They'll ruin my business going to fight when they know it's against the company. From now on they will cross further down river."

Freedom was amazed he thought maybe someone would find out what happened, but never expected there would be consequences. They got off and he went and signed his name.

"Mr. Burn wants to see you," he was told.

Freedom said, "Yes suh, Mr. Burn?"

"I hear that there was some trouble last night across the river." Mr. Burn said.

"No suh, Mr. Burn, just a misunderstanding. It won't happen again, suh." Freedom said.

"See to it that is doesn't. I'm running a business and if you people can't get along, I'll get some more boys to do the job. Is that clear?"

"Yes suh, Mr. Burn." Freedom replied and went to work.

Chapter 5
The Truth Will Set You Free

Freedom didn't see Jiles, but that was just as well. He had to keep his job. At break time one of the men Big Jim came up to him and apologized.

"I need my job, he said and Jiles said if I didn't come he would see that I was fired. I don't know what you did to make him so riled up, but I need my job."

Freedom said, "I don't hold no grudge. I need my job too, and walked away."

"Why did Jiles hate him? Was it because he called him Jiles the first day?" Wondered Freedom.

Little did Freedom know that Jiles' family knew Joshua the friend of his father Henry. They all thought that Henry had gone on to California. They had gotten reports over the years that he and Joshua were there working on ships. So when Freedom said that his father was Henry and he had been a slave, well Jiles knew he was lying. And he could not abide a liar. He felt that Freedom had fooled the boss and got special privileges.

Freedom decided to stay away from Jiles as much as possible. Freedom was beginning to learn a trade. He was very observant and each day he asked a few more questions. By the end of the month, Freedom was doing some hands on work.

One morning there was a buzz around the camp. Jiles did not show up for work. This was a rare occurrence. Mr. Burn didn't tolerate absences. There were a lot of speculations, but Freedom kept to his work and himself.

At the end of the day Mr. Burn told him to go find out why Jiles didn't come to work.

Freedom said, "yes suh," and started for home.

He crossed the river and went home. Johnny was there and he told him what Mr. Burn said.

Johnny said," let's go then before it gets dark."

The two set out for Jiles'. Jiles lived a ways down the settlement. Mostly coloreds lived on this side of the river. Some were free some former slaves. They had gone about an hour when they came to sturdier houses with some foundations to them. Freedom was surprised. Some had gardens, better than Mama Sara's, but not more loved. They even saw men dressed in suits, women in nice dresses. He never saw colored folk looking like white folk.

"Is this what his mama meant that things wouldn't always be like they were?" He wondered.

"What you looking at boy?" Startled Freedom.

He looked at a fair skinned colored man glaring at him and Johnny.

"You see a boy around here?" Johnny asked.

The man looked at him and mumbled something and walked away. Johnny asked a boy if he knew where Mr. Jiles lived. He pointed to a white clapboard house a little distance away. They walked there and knocked on the door. It was a modest house but clean. Mrs. Jiles answered the door. She looked pleasant enough, but worried about the eyes.

"Ma'am, my name is Johnny and this here's Freedom. He works with Mr. Jiles. Mr. Burn sent him to find out why he didn't come to work today."

"He's sick, and I've tried everything I know and the doctor comes only once a month to the job." She answered.

The men came in and went to the bedroom where Jiles was lying in the bed. He looked up, but was too weak to move.

Freedom looked at him and asked Mrs. Jiles to make a pot of hot water for tea. While she was putting the pot on to boil, Freedom took his pack off his back and rummaged around and found a smaller pack. In it was some herbs Mama Sissy had given him for all sorts of ailments.

He threw about a half a spoon into the water and when it boiled he told the misses to take it off the fire, cover it and let it simmer.

"When it cools give it to Mr. Jiles he will feel better in the morning."

They left and started back to the mill side of the settlement.

The next day, sure enough Jiles was back on the job. He approached Freedom during lunch and thanked him.

He asked him, "Why did you lie about Henry and then come and help me when I was sick?"

Freedom looked at Jiles and said, "I don't lie!"

Jiles just looked at him. Then he told Freedom what he knew of Henry. How he had worked with Joshua his uncle and left to go to California to work there with him. He even came to say goodbye to my parents.

Freedom stared and said, "He never made it. He was captured and sold!" He was a slave all those many years. He met my mama Sara and they jumped the broom. They had eight children all sold and taken away."

"I was the last born. He told me about this place and how he loved making ships. I came here after they died to learn his trade and maybe go to California and his home one day."

Jiles nodded and said," I'm sorry, Freedom. We all thought he made California. In fact some people said that they had seen him there. I thought you was lying."

He put his hand out to Freedom. Freedom took it and they shook hands.

"You have to come to supper one day so we can talk."

Freedom agreed and went back to his work helping shape the side bars of the ship and thought, "This is really the place that Poppa Henry lived and worked."

He finally felt some peace inside since leaving home. Freedom worked through to winter when they shut down because of the weather. It snowed something fierce there. He learned some trapping and skinning to help him and Johnny through the winter. He started back up come spring on into the next year. He was one of Mr. Burn's most reliable workers. He was a hard worker and learned really quickly. They were a busy ship yard.

Freedom had written Mary, but had not received a response. He wondered if she had met someone and married. He surely could understand that because it was very hard and dangerous for a woman alone.

Jiles came grinning up to him during lunch and handed him a letter. Freedom looked at him questioningly.

"Read it!" Jiles said.

Freedom read it. It was from a Joshua. He was the son of Henry's friend Joshua. He was inviting Freedom to come to California and see what his father had not had the opportunity to. Freedom looked at Jiles again.

Jiles said, “I came across an old address my father had and wrote Joshua and told him about you. This just came with the supplies.”

Freedom said, “As soon as I finish this job I’ll go.”

“Then write and tell them that you’ll come,” Jiles said.

Johnny and Freedom sat down to eat some beans and rice after a long days work. Johnny told Freedom about the mill and Freedom told him about the letter.

“You going to California?” Johnny asked.

“I am,” said Freedom. Soons the job is done in a few months. I done put a little money aside and can make it there I believe.”

“Yes suh, you can make it there. Just don’t go and forget ole Johnny.”

“I won’t Freedom, said. Why don’t you come with me?” He asked.

“Naw, this is my home. I’ll stay put but you can always come and visit me.” Johnny said.

Freedom told Mr. Burn that he was going to California. He stared at him like he was a madman.

“California! Who do you think you are? I gave you a

job treated you decently and you repay me by running off to California? Boy don't you know that I can have you arrested for anything I choose? Now get back to work and I don't want to hear anymore California nonsense from you. I don't know who filled your head with that trash. Get out and go back to work." Mr. Burn said.

Freedom was shocked. He never expected Mr. Burn to react like that. He didn't own him. He didn't even have to tell him that he was going. He was only trying to be fair and let him know that he would have to replace him. And now he was being threatened and treated like a slave. Freedom knew that he would leave sooner than he had planned. He walked slowly back to work. Almost everyone heard about what had happened. Most agreed with Mr. Burn.

Jiles came to him before he left for the day and told him, "You had better leave in the next few days. I hear Burn is planning on fixing you for trying to leave."

"Thanks, Jiles, I'll leave by the end of the week." Freedom said.

Chapter 6
Is There No Freedom for Me?

Freedom crossed over in silence and Collins watched him carefully. The word was already out. Freedom was going to pay.

As soon as he walked into the house, Johnny said, “I packed your things, here is some food wrapped in this paper. Get your stash and be on your way. Follow the path down to the mill and you can get a ride with Mr. Bill to the freight train and be on your way.”

“Johnny?” Freedom asked.

“I heard. Jiles sent word. You need to go tonight.” Johnny said.

Freedom thanked his friend took his bedroll and the food Johnny gave him. He went out back and got his money and started down the path to the mill. Sure enough Mr. Bill who delivered mail and supplies was waiting. They greeted each other and were on their way. Mr. Bill was a man of few words.

“Sorry Freedom, I hope California is better.”

"Thank you," Freedom replied.

They rode on in the wagon in more silence than talking. They finally arrived at the freight yard.

"I don't have to tell you to be careful. Choose your car carefully." Mr. Bill said.

Freedom hopped the freight. He settled in a car near the end. It was empty so he had to be careful. He thought on what had happened. He was sad to leave like he did. He really loved his work, but knew he had to go to California. He prayed while riding and decided to stop and see Mary first. If she was still free and had a mind to, he would marry her and then push on to California sending for her when he settled there.

This reverse ride was not as long as the ride up north. He remembered all the tricks of not getting caught. He finally got off in Mary's town. He made his way to the back path Mary had told him about. He saw her little house. It was still early, but he hoped he'd see her.

Freedom walked to her back door praying she wasn't married and knocked. Mary was in the kitchen cooking for her boarders. She wondered who would be knocking this early. She had no more room.

"Well, I guess if I have too I can give up my bed and make myself a pallet and sleep on the floor," she thought as she walked to the door.

Mary could not believe her tear filled eyes.

"Freedom is that really you?" She asked.

He walked in and took her hand.

"Yes, Ma'am it's me." He answered.

He watched as she wiped her eyes and sat down. Then she got up and walked to the little sideboard and picked up a letter and handed it to him. He looked down and saw that it was addressed to him. He sat down opened it and read it. Freedom looked at Mary. She had her back to him because she was cooking.

She said in the letter she missed him very much and didn't know how much longer she could stand waiting for him to come back for her. His eyes filled and he prayed thanking God for his coming now.

Mary took the food up and filled several plates and carried them to the small sitting room. Her boarders began to eat and laugh and talk. She came back into the kitchen and fixed Freedom a plate of eggs and ham with a biscuit. It was supposed to be her breakfast, but he was here and it didn't matter she could eat later. He just looked at her.

"Eat; I know that you had a long journey."

He blessed the food and started to eat. After he finished she told him he looked tired and should rest, while she finished with her boarders.

“There’s a little shack out back go and rest.”

Freedom wanted to hug her badly, but he said, “Thank you ma’am and left.”

The little shack was where Mary stayed when she had many boarders. Freedom unrolled his blanket. He lied down and fell asleep. He was dreaming of Mama Sara singing, he woke up and it was Mary singing. She was outside hanging clothes. Freedom lay very still and listened.

“Thank you Lord, thank you Lord, for loving me. Thank you Lord, thank you Lord, for dying on that tree. Thank you Lord, thank you Lord, for rising from the dead. Thank you Lord, thank you Lord, for coming back again.”
She sang beautifully.

Tears came to his eyes. He was so thankful for having met Mary. She was in his heart helping with the ache he had for losing his mama. Freedom got up and walked to the door of the shack and went outside to where Mary was hanging clothes.

“Looks like you have a house full.” He said.

She turned and smiled at him.

“Yes, I have been blessed to earn a living. I hope you were comfortable and rested well.”

“Yes ma’am, I did. I’m on my way to California.” Freedom said.

She stopped, turned and looked at him. He took her hands and led her to two stools she had in the small yard with her laundry basket. He put the basket on the ground and they sat down. He told her all about his journey north and the adventure of learning the trade and how the boss turned on him when he told him about California.

"I was planning on leaving in a month so I could have a little money, but I see now it was time for me to come. You remember when I came through before I told you that God had a plan and future for me? Well, you are a part of that plan, Mary."

"I knew on the ride back that I had to come to see you now and not after I got settled in California. I want to ask you to be my wife. I don't want to lose you. So will you please be my wife, Miss Mary? I don't have much but I did put some money aside and as soon as I get settled in California I will send for you."

Mary just stared at him. She loved him from the first. She hoped one day he would ask her to marry. Now, after missing him and realizing she couldn't go on alone, here he was asking her to marry him.

He stopped talking and looked at her.

"Yes, Freedom, I will marry you," Mary answered.

Freedom grinned and made a loud whooping yell. He grabbed her hands and danced a jig. They laughed. He asked her who would marry them. She said that she would ask her pastor Rev. J.L. Jackson if he would.

Freedom and Mary went to her pastors' home. He was chopping wood in his yard.

"Good morning, Rev. Jackson," Mary said.

He looked up and greeted her, and shook hands with Freedom.

"Come in," he said to them.

Inside Mary introduced Freedom to her pastor. She had told him about Freedom and her desire to marry him one day. He talked with them for awhile. Mary thanked him and left.

Freedom stayed and talked, sharing his life up to that point with the pastor. He agreed to marry them before Freedom left for California. He sent word for Mary to talk to the women at the church to help her prepare.

The ceremony was simple but very sacred to Freedom and Mary. The church members really loved Mary and made it a special day for them. Freedom stayed for several months with Mary. Every moment was precious to them. They made plans for their future. He left most of the money he had saved with her. He took just enough to keep him until he could find a job on his way to California.

Mary was concerned for his well being on his long journey. She sewed some of the money in his jacket lining and gave him a letter to read after he left.

Chapter 7
A Wife and a Vision

On his way again, Freedom paused to read Mary's letter as he settled waiting for the train. He chuckled, and thanked God for such a good wife. He prayed for her and his safety and soon reunion. He overheard some men talking about a wagon train going out west with supplies. It seems men paid a lot to get supplies from the east. It seemed that drivers and shotgun riders all were needed. Now Freedom wasn't a shot gun rider, but he had driven with Fred on his wagon and helped. He wondered how hard it could be.

He went back to the house and told Mary about it. They went to ask the Reverend about it. He told Freedom it was too dangerous. The men were always attacked on the long drive. Not many made it alive. Freedom decided to ride the rail and walk and hitch a ride with anyone going his way. He finally left and it was rough going but he made some friends along the way who helped him out. He traveled through the winter and the snow was heavy at times.

Freedom had learned how to spear fish as well as trap and skin when he was up north and that surely came in handy. He learned how to build a fire from Poppa Henry when he was home so he was able to care for himself pretty well. Thankfully he met a couple, the James' who needed help cleaning their barn and gathering wood and helping with their milking. He stayed with them for food and shelter for several months working and sleeping in their barn. He pushed on when there was a little clearing in the weather. His next work was tending cattle on a small ranch. He learned a lot even some branding.

Freedom finally hitched a job near the end of a cattle drive and reached Texas and joined another one to California. He got his pay and looked for a place to bunk down for the night. It was hot. He wondered is this how it was in my mama's home. There wasn't much shelter. He saw men on horses and some wagons whipping up dust.

He came upon a small settlement. Freedom went to the blacksmith's shop to find out where he was and where on earth ship yards were. To his surprise he wasn't a colored man. His name was Big Ray and he was hospitable. He asked Freedom a lot of questions. It was clear that he was lonesome.

Freedom stayed and helped him for about a month so he could eat and learn his way around in this California. He learned how to make horseshoes and shoe a horse, mule and anything else that needed shoeing. He was becoming quite handy with shoeing horses, but Big Ray was afraid he might take over his business.

Freedom had seen posters about a cattle drive, they were looking for drovers. One thing about a drive they didn't care what color you were as long as you did your job.

Freedom was mulling it over in his mind whether he should

sign on for the drive. He would have more money and he would be closer to his destination and not traveling alone. He could ride and now he could shoe a horse. He decided to sign up.

Freedom said good bye to Big Ray. He had bought a horse and saddle from Ray. The ones he used on the drive were not his. He got himself a hat with a wide brim for the sun and gloves. He traded his old boots for some California boots. He tied his bedroll to his saddle and put his food into the saddle bag and was on his way to join up with the herd.

Freedom was riding his horse named Courage and passing through another small settlement and he pulled up and looked in shock and disbelief. There was a colored man being whipped and no one lifted a finger to help him. In fact they were gathered around laughing. Freedom's first instinct was to run-over and try to break it up but he knew better. He rode over into the alley and waited and watched. When they had beaten the man they patted each other on the shoulder and went into what looked like a makeshift saloon. Freedom walked slowly over to the man to see if he was still alive. He was, Freedom gently lifted him and laid him on his horse in one swift movement. The man groaned in pain.

Freedom walked behind the building and mounted and rode out of the town. He doubled back and headed for the town he had left. He rode up to Big Ray who was shoeing a horse.

He looked up and said, "I thought you were headed for the cattle drive".

"I was, but I need to use the shack for a few days first," Freedom said.

Big Ray said, "Go right ahead."

He knew that something was up, but did not want to get in Freedom's business.

"Thank you suh," Freedom replied and walked around to the shack he had been staying in.

He gently took the man off of the horse and took him inside, laying him face down on the cot.

Freedom started a fire and put water on to get warm. He threw a handful of herbs into the water. He went and took the handkerchief that Mary had given him and put it in the water. Freedom gently cut the shirt off of the wounded mans' back. There was much crying out in pain from the man on the cot. Freedom cleaned the cuts as much as he could over the yells. Finally he put some ointment on the cuts and let him lie for a while uncovered. He knew that they needed some air.

He remembered the stories that his Poppa had told him about whippings.

Freedom knew that some men were still angry about the emancipation, but he never thought that he would see this. The man had passed out from the pain and exhaustion.

Freedom went and talked for a while with Big Ray. He went and got some food from the little Mexican cantina. He had taken a liking to some of that food. He got some beans homemade tortilla and rice for the man in the shack and returned to see if he had awakened.

Just as he was walking in the door he saw that the man was trying to get up.

"Hold on there, be careful or else you'll hurt yaw self." Freedom said.

"Who are you? How did I get here?" The wounded man asked.

"Calm yaw self down. Names Freedom, I was on my way to join up with a cattle drive when I came across you being whipped. I brought you here to try and help you get better."

Freedom pulled a stool close to the cot.

"Thank you, suh. I thought that I was going to die and was feared for my family all alone without me. Names Jackson, Robert Jackson. My wife and two young uns live on the other side of that little town you found me in."

"I had come to town to get my mule shoed and them men didn't like that I had a mule or was free. I tried to keep calm and walk away, but they surrounded me and started hitting me."

"All I could think of was my family alone and unprotected. I appreciate what you did for me but I can't stay here. I got to go and let them know I'm alive. I don't want my boy Junior to go to that town looking for me and get himself killed." Robert said.

"Settle down I'll help you. You need to eat a little for your strength. Let me give you one of my shirts to cover yourself. Gently, that's fine! Do you think that you can ride?" Freedom asked.

"Yes suh, I can. I have to!" answered Robert

"Wait here I'll get another horse and ride with you."

Freedom went and gave Big Ray his Poppa's watch for a horse and saddle.

"I'll be back to redeem them so don't sell them," he told Ray.

"If you come back I'll be here. But if I'm not they will be buried behind the shack." Ray said.

Freedom thanked Ray and left.

Jackson led the way slowly. He knew a way around the town in which he was beaten. Finally they came upon a small settlement. There were about a dozen small houses in a circle.

"That's the strangest thing I've ever seen," Freedom thought.

As they rode near people came walking towards them. They didn't look too friendly and had shotguns.

"Wait up," it's me said Jackson as he waved his hand.

They ran up to him and gently helped him down from the horse. His wife Anna came running crying with the children.

"I'm alright, but don't touch my back I been whipped."

They stopped and stared. They looked at Freedom. He stayed on his horse and looked at the men.

Chapter 8
Anesville a Town of Hope

"Names Freedom, I found him and brought him home," was all that he said.

"Welcome to Anesville, Freedom. Come on in and we will take care of your animals. Fine looking horse you got there," one of the town's men said.

"Thank you," Freedom answered.

Freedom followed the men into the town and watched as the horses were taken to a small smithy lean-to in the middle of the small town. He was taken to a church where he was given some food and water. They shared with each other their sojourn in this new land.

When they found out that Freedom could shoe horses they wanted to make him their smithy.

"No suh, thank you kindly but I have mission of my own." Freedom said.

"Did you ever think that mission was for your father and not you?" Jim one of the farmers asked.

“No suh, I never did,” Freedom answered.

Freedom sat down and ate with the Jackson’s. Mrs. Jackson was so grateful to him that she insisted. He ate some good victuals almost as good as his wife Mary’s.

“Why don’t you send for her and bring her here?” asked Mrs. Jackson.

“I told her that I was going to be a shipbuilder.” Freedom said.

“Well suh, this is a new country,” she said, so many old plans have to be let go of. It’s time for new ones.”

“My Robert here wanted to learn how to build houses proper like, Mrs. Jackson said. We decided to take a chance and come out west and help to build a town. Well we got here and he was treated the same as back home.”

“We met up with many more families who came for a better start and decided to put our lot together and build our own town. Here we are, Anesville it’s small but growing. We started with six families and now we have twelve. You should come on and join us Freedom.” Mrs. Jackson said.

“What did you do back home.” Junior Jackson asked Freedom.

“I helped my folks sharecropping. I read the Bible at church and sometimes preached a little when the circuit rider wasn’t there.”

"You can read and preach. We don't really have a preacher here." Junior said.

"But you have a church," Freedom said.

"Yes, replied Mrs. Jackson, we honor God and share what we remember together of how he took care of us in this unfriendly land. But we hardly have more than a few pages of the Bible.

Freedom will you read and preach for us before you head on out?" She asked.

"Yes ma'am."

The word spread like wildfire around the settlement. There was going to be a real service on Sunday.

Freedom bedded down in the little house that had been vacated by one of the men who had died. He prayed and thanked God for his journey so far. He was thankful for being able to help Robert and bring him home again.

He paused in his praying and then said, "God if you have brought me here to this place to stay and put down roots please let me know. You know my heart has been shipbuilding, but if that was for my Poppa and not me let me know. I want to do what you want for me, Amen."

Freedom rested very well. He was up early helping the men around the settlement clearing trees. He was strong and had learned up north at the shipyards. Freedom had a good appetite and ate some sausage, eggs and potatoes. Freedom was missing Mary a great deal. As long as he was traveling he was able to keep his longing for her down. But now that he was in a town and working with families and children he truly wanted her with him more and more.

Finally, on Sunday the people of Anesville came to the little church and sang many songs of thanksgiving and praise. Freedom was transported back to the little church he attended with Mama Sara and Poppa Henry. Tears came to his eyes.

He read from 1 Corinthians 13:11, "When I was a child I spoke as a child, understood as a child, I thought as a child; but when I became a man I put away childish things."

He began to preach on releasing the things of your youth and accepting what God has for you.

Freedom read on from Philippians 3:13 and 14, "Forgetting those things which are behind and reaching forward to those things which are ahead, I press toward the goal for the prize of the upward call of God in Christ Jesus."

During the service Freedom believed that the call on his life was genuine to be a preacher. He remembered all the old folks from home telling him that, but he wasn't sure then. Now he was and he also knew that his home was wherever Mary was. After the service was over Freedom knew that he was going to return for Mary.

Freedom sat and had supper with the Jacksons. He told Robert that he was going back for his wife Mary and would return as soon as they were able.

He stayed in Anesville for several months preaching, helping out the settlers with their plowing, and shoeing horses and mules. He found a site for his and Mary's home. He and several of the men cleared and area for the house he was going to build.

Freedom wrote Mary that he was coming home. He also wrote to Joshua to inform him that he would not be coming at that time. He thanked him again for the invitation and promised that when he returned with his wife Mary he hoped that Joshua would visit them in Anesville. He headed out for home.

Freedom left Anesville and headed back to return the horse and saddle to Big Ray. He got his poppas watch and bedded down for the night. At first light he started for home.

Chapter 9
Home Again

Freedom sat down with Mary and told her all about his journey and the people of Anesville, and his determination to be their preacher and homestead. He wanted her to come with him back there to start their lives together.

Mary was so happy to have Freedom home. She wasn't sure about Anesville. She wanted them to just sit still and be together for awhile. Freedom understood and just settled in at the boarding house. He reinforced the shack and made it livable for them. He went out every day and did odd jobs.

Mary had their first born a son. They named him Henry John for both fathers who had died. The boarding house was very busy, so Mary was able to make enough money to help out. Freedom continued to speak to Mary about Anesville. Freedom helped out with Pastor Jackson at the church.

Mary had another child they named her Sara Anne for their mothers. Freedom had now been home three years. He was a patient man. He continued to talk about the people of Anesville and the new start that was waiting for them. One morning after breakfast Mary said that she was ready to go; the children were old enough to travel.

Freedom and Mary told the congregation that they would be leaving at the end of April to have the warmest days for the journey. He heard of a wagon train traveling to California and planned to join with his family. Some people traveled by train, but many still went by wagon train. Mary needed to sell her rooming house, and the church decided to buy it so it would be still owned by coloreds.

Come April all the church members brought a dish and they had a dinner to say farewell to Freedom and Mary. Some even baked their special dish for them to take on the journey.

"You never know where you'll find something to eat on the way." Sis Janie said.

They stood in a circle and Rev. Jackson prayed.

They all hugged Freedom, Mary and the children and said, "Farewell, God be with you till we meet again."

Freedom, Mary and children headed home to the boarding house for the last time.

Freedom sat pensively looking out of the door.

Mary asked him, "Are you feeling alright Freedom?"

He was silent for what seemed like a long time. He turned his head slowly looking up into her face.

His eyes were moist, "yeah dear, I'm fine. I was just supposing."

“About what?” Mary asked.

“Oh, my brothers and sisters, you remember I told you Mama and Poppa had eight younguns sold out from under them to slavery?” I remember hearing my momma crying and praying for them. She wanted them to be safe and know that she loved them.” Momma Sara said that she never spected to see them again like her family, but prayed they were all safe.

“I was supposing what it would be like to meet them here and not wait till heaven,” Freedom said.

“Maybe you will, Freedom, maybe you will, Mary said. Come on to bed, it’s getting late and the children will be up early and ready for their adventure to our new home.”

“Go on along Mary, I’ll be there directly.”

The children, Henry John and Sara Anne were asleep. Mary looked in on them and sat remembering her past. Mary’s parents had died in slavery, never seeing freedom, but Mary was living it for them. Mary’s mother Anne died in childbirth or right after. She was taken by Mama Bess another slave woman with younguns of her own, wet nursed and cared for until she was old enough to fetch a good price and then sold off. Her father John had been a runaway, brought back and beaten mostly to death. He died later of his wounds.

Freedom, Mary and their children were the first in their families to be free in this new land. They had promised themselves that they would be true to God and to each other.

They packed up the wagon and hitched the two mules they bought with the money they got after Mary sold her boarding house. Mary had saved the money Freedom had left with her when he first headed for California. So they had a little nest egg for their new life. They prayed before they started on their journey.

Freedom said, “I believe we are going to see what Mama Sara was telling me about when I was a boy.”

Freedom, Mary, Henry John and Sara Anne climbed up into the wagon and started for Anesville, California, and their new life.

About the author

Sallie L. Betner Cupit is a widow, mother of three daughters and grandmother of seven, three girls and four boys. Graduated with a B.S. in Journalism, Temple University and a Master in Education, San Jose State University. She taught elementary school in San Jose, California for many years. Sallie has also served in Kenya and Tanzania as a missionary teacher.

She has enjoyed writing since childhood and continues to write.

Sallie lives with her daughter in Mishawaka, Indiana, and plans to return to Kenya early next year.

Sallia04@hotmail.com

CPSIA information can be obtained at www.ICGtesting.com
263578BV00001B/44/P
9 781456 069322